Brief Encounters

Stephen Baker

TSL Drama

Published in Great Britain in 2021
By TSL (Drama) Publications, Rickmansworth
Copyright © 2021 Stephen Baker
ISBN / 978-1-914245-11-4
Cover photo: https://pixabay.com/photos/wave-skimmings-ocean-spray-rock-1169899/

Rights of performance

Contents

Monologues for Men   page

Biker Girls	60 year old	3 mins	5
Lapping It Up	early 30s	4 mins	9
The Drive	early 60s	4 mins	13
Red Shoes	early 40s	10 mins	17

Monologues for Women

Yummy Mummy	late 30s	3 mins	25
Eastern Delight	early 60s	4 mins	28
Home Help	late 30s	4 mins	33
Bus Stop	early 50s	12 mins	37

Biker Girls

John is 60 and lives with his wife Gail.

Setting:
Armchair

Performance time:
4 minutes

John sits in a chair in the lounge of his house.

Lights up

Chris is a source of very useful information. If you want to know what is happening and where, Chris is your man. We've known each other for about 40 years now. I suppose I've come to rely on him to stimulate my rather dull boring life. Like most guys of my age, I've just turned 60 and married by the way, I'm always looking for a bit of excitement. Nothing that will get the missus, Gail, too worried. Just something that makes me feel young again. When I first started hanging around with Chris we burnt the candle at both ends, so to speak. Night clubs, parties and the odd strip club. Nothing was off limits. We just lived a very exciting life. But then I got married and he remained single.

Like a lot of married couples we have ups and downs and if I'm honest I feel in a bit of a rut, the nights revolve around the television, and an early night means that one of us has be up early in the morning for work. Don't get me wrong, I'm not looking for an affair, just a bit of excitement. Anyway, Chris had told me of a club he'd heard of where a gang of Hells Angels frequent and apparently they get biker girls to get up on the tables for an impromptu strip. It's all word of mouth. Anyway, we set off on the night to where Chris was reliably informed it was all to happen.

I've had this fascination with leather clad girls since I was a teenager in the 70s. I remember sitting down to watch *Top of the Pops* with my two older sisters and on came Suzi Quatro singing *Devil Gate Drive* and I was hooked. It was biker girls for me. Unfortunately, we lived in a small village in Norfolk and there weren't any biker girls there, only well turned out girls like Gail, who thought they were being rebellious because they didn't have their hair permed like their mother. Oh, how I yearned for a girl like Suzi Quatro. I used to dream that I would be at the school disco and the door would burst open and in would walk a leather clad blonde beauty, who would walk up to me and demand that I dance with her to rock and roll. She'd tell the DJ to get the Bay City Rollers off the turntable under threat of a beating outside, then we'd take centre stage and jive away, with me twirling her around my head and then swinging her through my legs. We'd

6

then leave with everyone staring at us and I'd climb on the back of her Harley Davidson, and off we would ride into the sunset.

Anyway, back to the strip joint. I told the wife, that we were going for a quiet drink and not to wait up. We got there in good time and sure enough, just as Chris said the place was packed with Hell's Angels. I've never seen such a wild bunch in all my life. I certainly wouldn't have wanted to argue with any of them. The place reeked of oil and bad odour. I don't think having a bath was a high priority to these guys. I thought to myself, I'm not sure what I'll tell the wife when I get in, that kind of smell gets onto your clothes. I'm sure I'll think of something, the car broke down seems probable.

I looked around to see if there were any leather clad women but couldn't see any. I thought they must be in a room somewhere getting ready to entertain the lads. I started to get really excited. The music was pounding away, The Rolling Stones, ZZ Top and Gun's N Roses. Real biker music. The tension in the bar was electrifying. You just knew that something was going to happen and then it did. Just as *Sweet Child of Mine* by Guns N Roses came on the jukebox this giant of a Hell's Angel got up on a table and said, 'And now for the night's entertainment, a live strip.' There was a loud cheer. He told the packed pub that he had chosen the person himself who would be the entertainment. We all waited in anticipation. He then pointed directly at me and said, 'It's him, the guy in the red jumper.' I just froze. I thought there must be some mistake. But then the throng of bikers started to part in the middle and create a path to a table, and they started to chant, 'strip, strip,' whilst clapping their hands.

I looked at Chris and said, 'what the hell's going on?' Chris turned to the barman and asked, 'what's going on here mate? I heard it was biker girls who provided the entertainment.' He replied, 'not tonight. This is the gay Chapter of the Hell's Angles. Last week it was the straight bikers. We like to be inclusive.' I turned to Chris and said, 'what am I going to do?' Chris put his jacket on and said, 'I don't know what you're going to do, but what I'm going to do is get the hell out here. I just hope for your sake that they don't want any afters.'

Pause

I just froze to the spot.

Pause

Then I heard Gail's voice: 'John. John.' And I felt her nudge me in the side. I shot up sweating like I'd been in a sauna. I looked around me

7

and saw that I wasn't in some dingy bar, I was in bed with Gail. It had all been a nightmare. 'Are you okay?' said Gail. 'You've been restless for the last hour or so, shouting and saying something about biker girls.' I said, 'yes love, I had a terrible nightmare that I was in a head on collision with a young female on a motorbike.' Sometimes, honesty is not the best policy.

Ends

Lapping It Up

Kevin is in his early 30s and married to Kris. They have two children. He is a manager for an electronics company.

Setting:
Chair

Performance time:
5 minutes

Kevin sits in his office, he is formally dressed in shirt and tie.

Lights up

Well I've managed to get myself into a right mess, and have dropped a good friend of mine, Frank, in it as well.

Pause

Head office have been really strict on sickness and have sent memo after memo out as regards dealing with employees who repeatedly go sick. Well in my department there is a young woman, Mel, who is a walking sick note. Her nickname is 'Blue Moon,' because you've more chance of seeing one than you have of seeing her. Also, there've been strong rumours that she has been moonlighting, but we have never been able to get evidence to corroborate this. Anyway, I've been trying to do something about it for months now. We can't just sack people as it has been known for employees to take the company to a tribunal and win. So we have to play the game to the rules, but it's not helped by the fact we are a strong union company. And the shop steward is not a man to mess with. Burns is his name, a right militant and very knowledgeable on employee rights. He has won a few cases at tribunals against the company.

Pause

Mel's a young attractive woman in her early 20s and is employed as a secretary. The administrator complains bitterly about her, she rings in sick then we get numerous sick notes from her GP. She's had every ailment known to man I think, and some not known. I've had her on sickness reviews and phased returns, which meant her doing shortened hours. Anyway after repeatedly warning her she took not the slightest bit of notice and carried on ringing in sick. I checked with my friend Frank in HR and he said that I had followed the procedure correctly and advised a formal meeting with him in attendance. I duly set one up. Mel turned up with Burns and we got the lot, him threatening to take the company to a tribunal and her breaking down sobbing. We decided to adjourn the meeting so that Frank could do the necessary paperwork. If I'm honest, because of the emotion of the meeting, I didn't want to inform Mel and Burns that we were dismissing her. Call it cowardice on my part if you want, but I think things would have really erupted in there if I had. Frank and I decided

during a break for lunch it would be wise to send her a letter informing her of our decision.

Pause

So I closed the meeting and informed her and Burns that we would
come to a decision in the next few days and we would write to her
accordingly. They accepted this and left the room quietly, which was
a relief. I looked at my watch and saw that it was late, well 6.30. I had
told Kris that I would be home as soon as I was free. The problem was
I didn't really feel like going home. I had been in the meeting all day
and felt a bit stressed. When I am like that I need to let my hair down
a bit. So I had a word with Frank and we decided to tell a bit of a white
lie to our other halves. We rang them and said that some complica-
tions had arisen in the meeting and head office had advised sorting it
out there and then rather than dragging it out. Kris thinks of everything. 'What about your dinner?' she said. You can't go without a
meal.' 'Don't worry about dinner,' I said off the top of my head, 'head
office are bringing something across.' Head office are the biggest
penny pinchers in the business, they wouldn't give you a cup of
coffee for free. They provide a vending machine and you have to pay.

Pause

Anyway it seemed to do the trick. Kris wasn't happy I'd been out over
the weekend to football and stayed out late, so she felt I should be
home with her and the kids. I did feel a bit guilty I have to say. But I
also wanted to go somewhere else after the meal. It was a surprise
for Frank. So anyway after we had appeased the wives we set off to
a nice little Thai restaurant that I had come across. We had a lovely
three course meal and drank orange juice so as not smell of alcohol
when we got in. You have to think of these things. I told Frank I had
a surprise for him and he looked all excited. I reached in my pocket
and produced two free complimentary tickets for a lap dancing club
that had just opened. The tickets were dated for that night. 'Where
did you get those from?' he said. I just patted the side of my nose, as
you do. 'Can I take it you want to go?' I asked. 'You bet,' he said
eagerly. So off we went.

Pause

We got in the place, ordered a couple of drinks, then sat at a table
and waited for the entertainment. We weren't going to stay all night.
It was only 8.30 and we decided we would get home around ten. It
would be perfectly feasible to say that we had worked until 9.30 and

then come straight home. Girls started coming out and dancing on the stages and some were on the poles. It was great. Then one girl came over to us and started gyrating right in front of us. She was wriggling her backside right in front of us. If I said I wasn't excited I would be lying. Frank looked like he was going to have a heart attack. She was really giving it loads. Then she turned around and looked straight at the pair of us and smiled. It was Mel. She looked stunning. She always looked good when she attended work, as rare as it was, but she looked absolutely fantastic up there on the small stage. I looked at Frank and he looked at me and then we looked back at her. She then leaned over and said, 'check out the CCTV boys,' and then proceeded to rub her breasts in my face. She just got more and more provocative. She ended up sat in Frank's lap.

Pause

To be honest, I was relieved when she left us alone. Well I thought, it is true she has been moonlighting. We got out of there sharpish. Then Frank became very vocal, 'just where did you get those complimentary tickets from?' he said. 'They were in my in-tray after lunch.' I said. 'And correct me if I'm wrong, but didn't you let Mel and Burns use your office to prepare for the meeting?' he said. 'Yes,' I said sheepishly. I knew I'd been hit with a sucker punch. I simply couldn't win now. If we dismiss her, the footage of us being somewhere we shouldn't would get us into hot water with our other halves, if she isn't dismissed she will continue to ring in sick whenever she feels like it. And eventually head office will deal with me. And poor Frank will go as well.

Pause

Well, she certainly lapped it up and rubbed our noses in it. Literally, in fact!

Ends

The Drive

Paul is in his early 60s. He is married to Karen.

Setting:
Armchair

Performance time:
5 minutes

Paul sits in a chair in the lounge of his house.

Lights up

I'm a keen gardener and I just love the spring. It's a time for planting to give nature the chance to bloom. It was a Sunday, and I'd spent all day in the garden planting bulbs, mowing the lawn and generally preparing the garden for the summer. Then for the evening the plan was to relax. After the evening meal I showered and sat on the sofa relaxing. It was about 6 p.m. and I was just about to open a few cans of Special Brew, when Karen my long suffering wife came into the lounge with the telephone in her hand. I must admit I never heard it ring, but then I was lost in my own little world of listening to my vinyl collection of 70's music. The sort of thing we recycled teenagers do when we can.

Karen whispered, 'It's Dave.' Dave is my understudy at work. He's just turned 18 and has been taking driving lessons. He looks on me as a bit of a father figure, his natural father left when he was a toddler. When I answered the phone, he informed me that he is taking his driving test later in the week and asked if I would do him a massive favour and take him for a dummy run. He said if we go on a Sunday evening there would be less traffic on the road and he would be able to practise his manoeuvres.

Pause

I reluctantly agreed. Good job I didn't have any of my beer. I drove to his house, and we switched seats and set off on what was to be a very eventful journey. It was Dave who decided the route. He drove along the same roads his instructor took him down, but that was daytime not evening. As we were driving on a main road I noticed several women on the pavement looking at us. Then we stopped at traffic lights and that's when it happened. As the car was stationary, we were joined by two young ladies who opened the back doors and climbed onto the back seat. One of them said, 'when the lights turn green take the first left.' 'She sounds like a driving examiner. I wanted realism for my test and I've got it,' said Dave. 'This is no laughing matter,' I said. 'We have been well and truly compromised, and it could get worse.' Dave stopped the car when instructed to do so. I tried to explain the best I could that we were on a dummy run for a

14

driving test and not looking for a sexual encounter. 'Not our problem,' said one of them. 'It'll cost you £30 each whether we stay in the
car or not. No money and we scream the place down. The choice is
yours.'

Pause

I was just speechless. I really didn't know what to do. I looked at Dave
and he was on his mobile texting someone. I said, 'this is no time to
be texting anyone, and have you got any money? Because I haven't.'
I had left my wallet at home. Dave just looked at me and said, 'no,
sorry mate, I never thought. I put enough petrol in the car to go for
the drive, but I have no money on me, only loose change.' 'Well we
are well and truly up to our knees in the brown stuff,' I said. Just then
my mobile rang. It was Karen. I hesitantly answered. 'Hello,' I said
quietly. I thought if I have to ask her to bring £60 to the red light
district I am going to die of embarrassment. The ladies in the back
were getting impatient. One said, 'are we going to wait all day or
what?' 'We've got work to do, we're busy people.' I said, 'just be
quiet will you. I'm trying to talk to the wife.' 'Who's that you're
talking to?' said Karen. 'I can hear a woman's voice.' 'It's Dave,' I said,
he's talking to a woman he knows.' 'Are you okay?' she said. 'You
sound agitated. Is something wrong?' 'No love. Nothing's wrong,' I
said, with trembling in my voice. 'Well it doesn't sound that way to
me. You seem very agitated. You're not in any trouble are you?' 'No,'
I said. 'Well it doesn't sound that way to me.' She should have been
a detective the missus, she can smell a problem a mile off.

Pause

I was just about to pluck up the courage to tell her the bother we
were in when she said, 'and you know what day it is today or have
you forgotten?' My heart skipped a beat. I thought it was our wed-
ding anniversary and I'd forgotten it. If I wasn't in enough trouble
already. 'Well, we're waiting,' said a voice again from the back of the
car. 'I don't know love,' I whispered. 'She can't hear you,' said one of
the ladies. 'I can't hear you,' said Karen. 'I don't know love,' I said. I
knew it wasn't our anniversary, that was much later in the year, 10th
October to be exact. 'Is it the anniversary of when we met?' 'No,' she
said, 'try again.' 'I don't know love, and I'm really not thinking straight
at the moment.' 'He's not thinking straight,' echoed from the back.
'That's that woman's voice again. I hope you're not playing away
Paul,' she said. 'No I'm not playing away,' I said. 'Well I should hope
not,' she said. 'Well I'm waiting.' 'I honestly don't know love,' I said,

15

exasperated. 'If I've forgotten something important I'll make it up to you. I promise.' 'That's what they always say,' said a female voice from the back. 'I'll say you've forgotten something important,' Karen said. 'What?' I said. 'It's April fool's day,' she said. The whole car erupted in laughter. I looked around and Dave and the two women were in stitches. They were all in on it. It turned out Dave knew the two women, they lived near him, and he and Karen had come up with the idea to set me up for a prank.

Pause

I nearly died. But what a relief.

Ends

Red Shoes

Thomas is in his early 40s, he is married to Harriet. They have no children. Thomas is a serving police officer. His current role is working at the local police station in the lost property department.

Setting:
Scene One: Police Station: office chair
Scene Two: Local Park: bench
Scene Three: Lounge: chair

Performance time:
10 minutes

Scene One

Thomas sits in the police station lost property office where he works. He is in his police uniform.

Lights up

I knew when I was placed in the lost property office that I would find it difficult and I was not wrong. But I had no say in the matter, it was the 'powers that be' who made the decision. It was an incident last year that prompted the move. I had been working in the traffic section for about ten years and really enjoying it. Well I say enjoying it, it was okay. There were ups and downs. Then when I became a sergeant I was also transferred to a special unit: Police Interceptors. This was the elite drivers from our section who were given new supped up cars, and our job was to go after the bad guys in high speed chases. Well I've always had an adrenaline rush. I jumped at the chance to drive really fast cars very fast.

Pause

I had been in the unit for about six months and getting a real buzz from the job. I was renowned for being one of the best drivers. I usually worked on my own, well with my dog, Tyson. I liked it like that. Tyson was always there as back up. We caught a lot of bad guys, we did. I turned up for the late shift one evening and was told there was to be a briefing. I went along with all the others from the unit. The inspector informed me that I was to have a young woman police constable, Gina, with me for the shift. I was not best pleased, it has always been me and Tyson. That shift was the beginning of a downward spiral, as an embarrassing issue came to the fore.

Pause

[*Takes a deep breath*] I have a foot fetish. Female feet that is. The young PC was known to me, I had seen her previously and I have to say, she's got a lovely pair of feet. Anyway, she got in the car and we started our patrol. I was driving, she was in the passenger seat. I tried to remain focused, I really did. But I just couldn't help keep glancing at her beautiful feet. There they were resting so elegantly on the car mat, inside a pair of very elegant black boots. I could feel my glance getting more and more drawn to her feet. I had to tell myself to concentrate. We talked a bit, but when she was on the radio taking information from control I could see her feet moving from side to side, it was just too much. I felt myself looking more and more. I heard her say that we had a call to attend a car theft from a private property. The theft was in progress.

Pause

She was giving me the directions and I was putting my foot down, and had the blue lights and sirens going. I was telling myself to keep looking where I was going and not to glance down at her feet, because we were now travelling at some speed. I tried, I really did. But the urge was too great. I glanced down to see her feet move just slightly. Then I heard her scream, 'Sarg, look out!' It was too late. I lost control of the car and we careered through a garden fence and into a garden pond, it was pandemonium. The air bags came out, as did the owners of the property. I heard a woman shout, 'there's a police car in my pond.' I checked Gina was okay. She was a little shaken but apart from that she was okay. Unfortunately two fish weren't so lucky.

Pause

I had to report to the inspector about the incident, and fill in a statement. I said that I had just lost control, I put it down to the wet conditions. It had been raining a bit. Unfortunately, Gina had also been asked to put a statement in and she put that she noticed I kept becoming distracted, and that she didn't like to comment as I was her superior and she was new to the job.

Pause

The result was I was demoted to police constable and transferred to lost property. Now I face the real chance of losing my job and pension as well. I am to face a disciplinary hearing. I am waiting for my representative from the police federation. After the incident in the police car, I knew I had to be on my very best behaviour. But, unfortunately temptation got the better of me. My foot fetish came to the fore once more.

Pause

Every weekend we would get a plethora of female shoes handed in after the wearer no doubt got drunk and took them off for comfort. So, they would find their way into the lost property office. I would have to sign them in and place them on a shelf awaiting collection from the owner. One shift a beautiful pair of red high heel shoes came in. I just couldn't help myself looking and touching them. In the office I would be working with female civilian staff. What I didn't know was that they were keeping a file on me. Every time I went into the back office to look at the shoes, they recorded it. Apparently, a senior officer had requested they did this. I was under suspicion after one of the staff had noticed me touching pairs of high heels constantly throughout the day. She took her concerns to an inspector.

Pause

I was on duty one day and was summoned to an office where two officers from AC 12 were in attendance. AC 12 are the internal investigating officers. I was informed that a representative from the police federation was arriving as I was to be spoken to. When he came I had no idea what it was about. Then we got into the room and were informed of the allegations and I was served with a disciplinary notice. That was last week. I have had to work with the people who have basically been spying on me. It's been awful. And of course I've had to tell the wife. She's been supportive. But I'm not sure how she'll react if I'm found guilty and sacked.

Gets up and walks to the door.

Fades

Scene Two

Thomas sits on a park bench. He is smartly dressed in a suit and tie.

Lights up

Well who would have thought a pair of red shoes would cost someone their job? In my case they just have. I've just come from the disciplinary hearing and am finished. I've come to the park to get my head together before I head home to break the news to Harriet. She won't take it well. She'll more than likely walk over it. She's a lawyer, she has her career to think about. She's just started at a solicitors and she won't want this embarrassment affecting her promotion prospects. It'll be far better for her to cut all ties. I do actually understand.

Pause

So what happened in there? Well, I'll tell you. There were two hearings, the first was to establish the facts and decide on guilt; and the second was to accept any mitigating circumstances to take into consideration. I have just attend the latter. The first was cut and dried really. The three civilian women had kept a dossier on me. I work only with one of them at any one time. But because their statements were saying the same thing, I really had no defence. They all appeared in person and said that they had seen me on several occasions go into the back office and remove the shoes off the shelf and caress them. It was difficult to argue a case. My rep questioned all three of them but they had kept a record, and all three said that I made them feel uncomfortable. I was asked why I needed to keep observing the shoes. I answered that I needed an accurate description. 'You needed to look twenty times in one shift and eighteen another, then twenty-two times the next day?' said the investigating officer. I was beaten and I knew it. Then came the worst evidence. They had been monitoring my computer activity and provided evidence of my frequent Internet searching for sites relating to women's shoes. There was no defence I could give, I was 'bang to rights.' At that point my rep asked for an adjournment.

Pause

He basically told me that the case was overwhelming. He advised coming clean about my fetish. He asked me if there was anything in my past that I could bring in that might help my case. That's when I had a flash of inspiration. When I was at school I was referred to an education psychologist. I had been caught leaving the PE lessons half

21

way through and going into the girls' changing rooms so that I could view their shoes which were neatly placed under the changing bench. A teacher had followed me in and apart from scolding me, reported the matter to the head teacher. I was seen about it and when I said I liked looking at girls' shoes, I didn't actually think there was anything odd about it, they referred me to an education psychologist. 'Great,' said the rep, 'there will be a report. You have to get it.' I contacted the local education department and asked for my record and unbelievably they had the report. I obtained a copy and gave it to my rep. He argued in the second hearing that I was ill and that I needed help not punishment. It did the trick. Instead of sacking me, I have been allowed to retire on ill health grounds. That way the media won't get hold of it, it is all hush hush.

Pause

I still think the wife will divorce me.

Gets up and walks away.

Fades

Scene Three

Thomas sits in the lounge of his home. He is casually dressed.

Lights up

Well here I am after the biggest turnaround in my life. No longer a police officer and minus a wife. As I suspected, Harriet decided to seek pastures new. She said she wanted to make a new start for herself and I don't really blame her. At the law firm she has joined she has been given casework defending people. It would be a bit awkward if she was up against an officer who worked with me, you only needed for someone to say something. It was all round the station what I'd been up to. You can't keep anything under wraps in the police. Also, she has started seeing one of the other lawyers at the firm. She hasn't been awkward, she could have been. She accepted a reasonable financial settlement which has meant I've kept the house. We've been grown up about it all.

Pause

After all the ordeal, I started seeing a therapist through my GP. He was seeing me at the house. Fat lot of good that was. I dealt with social workers and the like whilst in the Force. Or the 'Duffle Coat Brigade' as we called them. I just knew when I made the appointment that some guy in a duffle coat would turn up at the house, probably sporting a beard, and I was 100% correct. We talked over a cup of tea for about an hour once a week for about four weeks. At the end of the course of therapy he submitted a report and what a surprise, he came to the conclusion that I have a foot fetish. Well what a shock that was! You could have knocked me for six. Anyway the only good thing was he encouraged me to do what Harriet had done and move on.

Pause

So, I joined a dating agency online. I had a couple of dates, but they weren't really for me. We didn't click, so to speak. But then I got in touch with this woman, Joyce they call her. Lives about five miles away. I met her for a coffee only last week. We really hit it off talking away about this and that. Then she said, 'can I ask you a personal question?' I said, 'fire away.' She said, 'do you have any guilty pleasures?' I thought for a bit and replied, 'yes. I have every Boney M song they've ever made.' Which is true actually. She just laughed. Then she said, 'do you want to know my guilty secret?' I said, 'yes, do tell. I'm all ears.' She said, 'you promise you won't laugh or run away.' 'Scouts honour,' I said. 'Because,' she added, 'my husband left me over it.' I said, 'I'm sure it will be fine. Whatever it is.' There was a long pause and she said, 'I am a compulsive buyer of shoes. I have hundreds of them, some still in boxes and some have never been worn. From trainers to high heels and flat shoes. The lot. I've got them all. Cost a fortune. What do you think of that?'

Pause

I reached into my pocket got my wallet out. Pulled out my credit card, put it on the table and said, 'a woman can never have enough shoes.'

Ends

Yummy Mummy

Vikki is in her late 30s and is married to Gary. They have one child, and live in the North East of England.

Setting:

Park bench

Performance time:

4 minutes

Vikki sits on a park bench. She is in sporting attire.

Lights up

Well that's another gym session done with and I don't think I can face going back. I was really enjoying the workouts and the get together afterwards with the girls. But given what has just happened, I don't think I can ever go back.

Pause

I expect you're wondering what this is all about. Well, I'll tell you. Me and Gary have been going through a bit of a rough patch in our marriage. The physical side of the relationship has taken a bit of a dive since I gave birth. Then Gary made a comment about my figure and the fact that I have put on a few pounds recently. He's alright, he has a manual job on a building site which keeps him fit. I am at home all day looking after the young one, and I don't get the time to exercise. Anyway, I was hurt by the comment. I went up a dress size that's all, but to him it was a huge issue. He kept going on about how slim I was when we met. I said, 'Gary, that was twelve years ago. And the weight that I put on was as a result of having your child.' Anyway I decided to do something about it. I told Gary that I will go to gym weekday mornings if he pays for a cleaner to come and clean the house twice a week and if Liam who is 18 months now can go to a nursery. He agreed. I have set my goal to get back to my original weight and be a 'Yummy Mummy.'

Pause

So I not only joined the local gym but enrolled on some of the keep-fit classes, zumba, spin and circuit training. I got in with a load of other girls and it was just great. After a session we would relax having a coffee in the café area. There'd be about five of us just having a real giggle. One of the girls, Fiona, was the centre of attraction. She would tell us all what she'd been up to between classes. She's a real beauty, with a figure to die for. She's just recently divorced and is living a very full single life again. Basically she has loads of guys on the go. Including one of the coaches, who must be all of twenty. Apparently, they've been having liaisons when the gym closes and he's got the keys. She's got a married business man whom she calls her 'sugar daddy.' The list is endless. After every class we get all the details.

26

Pause

I must admit I was very envious. Me and Gary just don't do it anyway near enough. Hence me joining the gym in the first place. I joined the gym to lose weight to improve things with Gary. Anyway, this morning was circuit training, which is my favourite class. The coach is the one who Fiona is involved with, amongst many others. After the gruelling session all five of us headed for the showers, got changed and met in the café. We are all sat there drinking our coffee when we get Fiona's love life as the topic of conversation. I thought we'd heard it all. She's apparently met a couple more guys online this time and has already bedded both of them. Not at the same time I might hasten to add, but with that one nothing would surprise me. She starts giving every detail of the first one she met, Dave. He is six feet tall and a body builder. We got every detail imaginable, where they did it, how long it lasted, the positions, the lot.

Pause

Then she starts telling us about the second guy. She said, 'he told me his name is James but I don't believe him, he doesn't look like a James. Far too masculine for a James. James is a name for the "boy next door type" not a brute like this,' she said. I replied, 'well if he's married he may not give you his real name.' 'Maybe not,' she said. 'I really don't care. With a body like that he could be called Rupert for all I care.' I said, 'so what was his body like if you don't mind me asking?' She said, 'On his chest he has a giant eagle stretching right across,' then she grabbed the spoon we'd stirred our coffee with and pretended she worked for NASA and was talking about the moon landings she said, 'Houston, the eagle has landed.' All the other girls were laughing hysterically. Then she said, 'and he's obviously a Newcastle United fan as he has Alan Shearer on his back.' One of the girls, Carol said, 'my brother has both them tattoos but I know it's not him you've been with because he's gay.' Another girl, Jules, said, 'most men in the North East have Newcastle United tattoos.' Then Fiona said, 'and he's got Newcastle United till I die across his navel.' Jules replied again, 'nothing unusual in these parts, it's practically obligatory where I live. Does he have anything that is not about Newcastle United?' To which she said, 'yes he has a dragon running all the way down his right leg with some wording coming out of its mouth. I can't make out what it says but I am rather distracted.' Everyone laughed except me. I said, 'I think I can help you there it says, "made in Newcastle, 3 September 1977".' I picked up my bag and left.

Eastern Delight

Janice is in her early 60s. She has been married to Frank
for 40 years.

Setting:

Armchair

Performance time:

5 minutes

Janice sits in her lounge. She is smartly dressed.

Lights up

Mother always said that you can never really know another person. No matter how long you've known them, there will be something about them that will surprise you. Everyone has a skeleton in the cupboard, she always said. I guess that's true about me and Frank. I've no skeletons in my cupboard. Frank knew everything about me. There wasn't much to tell really. We met at a school disco, started going steady, broke up when we were nineteen and then got back together again six months later and wed in our early twenties. In the six months we were apart I dated a couple of guys, but nothing serious. Frank was my only boyfriend really. The only one I ever loved.

Pause

In the forty years we were married we only spent four weeks apart, and that was when he went into hospital to have a pacemaker fitted. We had our ups and downs like every couple. But we always patched it up. We never went to bed angry with each other. When he was in hospital I visited him every night. We were so pleased to see each other. Everyone in the ward would look at us and comment how close we were.

Pause

I never had cause to doubt Frank, if you see what I mean. He could be a bit of a charmer where the ladies were concerned. If we went out anywhere he would engage in conversation with other women. I didn't get cross or feel threatened by it. He was generally just being friendly, it was his way. I never felt that he would run off with anyone else. I always felt he would be faithful.

Pause

Anyway, the operation seemed to give him a new lease of life. Before the operation he always seemed to be tired. Falling asleep in front of the telly, that sort of thing. Our love life took a bit of a nose dive. The consultant saw us both just before the operation and we did discuss sex. He said that some men who had the operation rediscovered their libido. Well, let's just say, that's what happened in Frank's case. [*She smiles*]

Pause

Everything went back to normal and I thought we were both happy with that. But something happened with him. He started to act differently. He was staying out late some evenings and could sometimes be a bit moody. I wasn't sure what the problem was, I would ask him if there was a problem and he always said, 'no'. So I took it that there wasn't. I did notice something very odd with his skin though. He always had very dry skin but it felt very oily at times. I mentioned it to him and he said that it was the blood circulating around the body better since the operation. I put my concerns to the back of my mind. On the whole everything was fine. But then there was the news that turned my life upside down.

Pause

I'd become used to Frank staying out late. We agreed that he could go out some evenings and I on other evenings. We didn't feel that we needed to live in each other's pockets. On this particular evening he said he was meeting up with a friend from work in a pub. I was sat on the sofa watching TV when there was a knock on the door. I went to answer it and there in front of me were two police women. 'Mrs Dawson?' asked one of the women. I said, 'yes, what's happened? Is it Frank?' 'I think it's best we talk inside,' said the other one. I invited them in, my heart was pounding. They came in, sat down and I just knew he was dead. I thought it was a car accident, I thought he'd had a heart attack at the wheel. There was an unbelievable silence, then one of them said, 'Mrs Dawson we have some bad news, I'm afraid your husband Frank has died.' I said, 'was he involved in an accident?' They both looked at each other and the other one said, 'no, he died peacefully.' 'Died where?' I said. 'Watching television,' said the other. 'Watching television.' I said, 'where was he watching television? Was it in a pub?' There was another long silence. 'No,' came the response. I said, 'was he in someone's house?' 'Not a house,' was the response. 'Not a house, well where?' I said. I knew he wasn't a member of any club because he just wasn't into that sort of thing, golf and tennis not his thing really. 'In a club,' one of them said. 'What club?' I said. It was like pulling teeth. 'A massage club,' was the response. I said, 'what do you mean, a sports massage club? He doesn't play sports.' 'No,' said one of them, 'not that sort of a massage facility. It was a female run business.' 'You mean a sex club?'

I said. 'Well possibly,' she muttered. 'Possibly,' I said. 'Either it was or it wasn't.' She looked embarrassed, the poor girl. Only a slip of a girl. The other one piped in, 'It's a massage parlour in the next town, there have been reports that extra services are given for a fee, but nothing has ever been proved.' I just sat there dumbfounded. Then it made sense, the oily skin. He'd been having oil rubbed into his skin by a female masseur, and then more than likely having sex with her; and this has been going on for weeks. I asked again about the TV watching. I said, 'so you are telling me he died in the waiting room of this massage parlour watching TV?' 'Correct,' said one them. 'It seems very strange to me,' I said, 'why would someone come off the street and sit in a massage parlour waiting room and watch TV?' 'He might have been waiting to be called for his massage,' said one of them.

Pause

Anyway they finally left. I was told where he was resting so I could pay him a visit. I went to bed early and cried myself to sleep. I felt so sad that I couldn't have been there at the end, and that someone else was, a girl he probably didn't even know well. I had been with him for over forty years.

Pause

I went to the local hospital's mortuary and asked to see Frank. They had put him on a table. Something struck me straight away as soon as I saw him. He had a smile on his face. It was the same smile I'd seen so many times after we had shared intimacy. He always had a smile on his face afterwards. I knew there and then the TV story was a pack of lies. I reckon he'd been having fun with a girl and it had been too much for him. The silly old fool. In a way I felt relieved. It would have been dreadful if it had happened to us. I felt a bit guilty about feeling that way.

Pause

The next day I did something that probably most women in my position wouldn't do. The police officers had given me the name of the place he visited, *Eastern Delight*. I drove down there out of curiosity. I wanted to see the place where Frank had spent his last few moments on this earth. I got there and stood outside just look- ing. It was about two o'clock in the afternoon and this must be when some of the girls start work. As I could see about five Asian looking girls enter the premises, I thought to myself: it's possible it was one of those girls who was with Frank when he died. I bet she panicked and told the management, and then they will have come to the room, got him dressed and removed him to the waiting room so the police wouldn't class it as a suspicious death.

Pause

I was feeling really sad, but then something made me give a wry smile. The name of the place *Eastern Delight* was lit up and underneath in a strap line it said: 'Good guys go to heaven, but bad girls take you there.' I just couldn't help but see the irony in it. I thought of the girls I had seen entering the premises and then I thought of the smile on Frank's face in the mortuary. And I thought, whoever it was who was with him at the end she certainly did her job.

Ends

Home Help

Ann is in her late 30s and divorced. She lives with her ten year old son, Sam. She has just lost her job as a home help.

Setting:

Armchair

Performance time:

5 minutes

Ann sits in her lounge. She is casually dressed.

Lights up

Everything started four months ago when I became a home help. I was a bit short of money after the divorce and a bit bored as well, really. It was difficult getting anything as I hadn't worked as such since I got married. I became a mum and a housewife overnight. From the bliss of the honeymoon to the drudgery of the kitchen and dirty nappies.

Pause

Anyway, I got a job as a home help. It was minimum wage, but the hours suited. I could work it around picking up Sam from school. I was assigned a few clients, and my job basically was to go round to their house and clean and run a few errands if needed. Nothing too demanding. I quite enjoyed the work. I say enjoyed, as I have just been dismissed for gross misconduct. Am I a bad person? I'll let you decide.

Pause

I bet you're thinking she's one of those people you read about in the papers, caught stealing from old people. No I wasn't. Although money did come into it.

Pause

The issue relates to one of my clients, an old gentleman named Tom, a widower. His wife had died a few years ago. Tom is in his late 70s with all his faculties, but had suffered a stroke, which had affected him physically. He struggled to walk mainly. Hence the need for home help. I went round once a week and cleaned for him. It was whilst I was doing the cleaning that I noticed his gaze. I could sense he was looking at me in a sexual way. I just ignored it really, got on with my job. Then he started passing comments. Pleasant ones, nothing smutty. Just compliments. He'd tell me that I had a nice figure and that I was attractive. The sort of things we women like to hear. I certainly didn't hear it from my ex, which is why he is my ex. Then he started telling me about his wife and how he missed her. I learnt that they still had an active love life up until she died. Which I thought was nice.

Pause

Anyway, as time went on Tom seemed to be more and more fixated with me, and if I'm honest I didn't discourage him. Then one time I could sense his gaze again, but I also sensed that he was not just content with looking, he was doing something whilst he was sat in his chair. I pretended I was unaware and carried on with my dusting etc. When I got home, I discovered I had a £20 note stuffed in my coat pocket. He must have put it in there as a kind of token, I guess. The rules state that no gifts of any kind should be accepted. But it was coming up to Sam's birthday and I thought well it will come in handy. I was really struggling to save up for a present for him. I don't like him to go without, even though money is tight.

Pause

When I went to Tom's again I never mentioned the money. I just got on with things, and the same thing happened again. I got home and discovered I had £20 in my pocket. I thought well if that's what he wants to do I don't see any harm in it. He never asked me to do anything and I never felt threatened. I just pretended not to notice. I have to say that I also started to wear more tight fitting clothes and sometimes lingered a bit longer in the lounge where he sat in his armchair. This behaviour doubled the gift. I was feeling really okay about things. I had more money to spend on me and Sam and Tom was enjoying himself. I really don't see where the harm was.

Pause

But then it happened. I went to his house again this time wearing the tightest pair of jeans imaginable. With the extra money I bought myself a pair of skinny jeans that I had had my eye on for some time. Unfortunately, it was all too much for him. I was bent over dusting the TV stand and could sense he was doing what he generally did and then I heard him groan and then there was silence. I just froze on the spot. I said, 'Tom, are you okay?' Silence. After about a minute I plucked up the courage to turn around. He was laid to one side in his chair, his head slummed forward with his trousers wide open. I went over and checked his pulse. There was nothing. I managed to stay calm and rang my boss. She told me to ring for an ambulance, which I did. She also told me not to touch him. I disobeyed. I couldn't leave him with his fly undone. I basically ensured he was decent, if you see what I mean, zipped his trousers and fastened his belt.

Pause

The ambulance and the police arrived about the same time. I had to give a statement to a woman police officer. I just said that I was cleaning and heard a groan and when I got to him he was dead. The police officer seemed perfectly content with everything. I had to explain to my boss what had occurred, she asked me to come to her office. I made sure that I went home and changed first before I went. I didn't want her to see me in my skinny jeans. I slipped on a baggy pair of jogging bottoms I wear for other clients.

Pause

I carried on working after that and actually never really gave the matter another thought. But then disaster struck. Apparently, the woman police officer was suspicious of me. She felt I was dressed inappropriately and had stated as such to her superiors. Unbeknown to me, she had liaised with my boss and they had compared notes. When it was apparent I had changed my attire to report to my boss they investigated things. It was discovered that Tom had been drawing money out of his bank on the day of my visit, by getting a neighbour to go to the bank for him; and their suspicions led the police to request that his body be swabbed, let's just say I should have bathed him.

Pause

Then the real hammer blow came. He had only changed his will. Before I came on the scene he had made a will leaving everything to his two daughters, who incidentally, never bothered with him. But without me knowing he had changed his will, leaving everything to me. His daughters were livid. I was interviewed at the police station accompanied by my solicitor. I explained that I did not engage in anything, which technically I didn't. It's not against the law to wear tight skinny jeans. After a few weeks of worry and sleepless nights I was finally told that the police would not be charging me with anything. Unfortunately, my boss was of the opinion that I had breached the strict code of conduct of the company. I was disciplined and sacked, with immediate effect.

Pause

But the will still stands. The daughters have tried to challenge it but failed. I will get everything, the house, his savings, the lot.

Pause

Glad I took the job actually.

Gets up from the chair.

Ends

Bus Stop

Stephanie is early 20s, attractive, brunette and single.
She works in an office.

Setting:
Scene One: Work staffroom: chair
Scene Two: Lounge: armchair
Scene Three: Bus shelter: bench
Scene Four: Hotel lobby: sofa

Performance time:
12 minutes

Scene One

Stephanie sits in the works staffroom.

Lights up

Well, here I am about to start another day in the office. I must admit I do get bored with this job, I really do. It's the routine that gets me down, seeing the same people all the time and just doing the same thing, day in, day out. Every week day morning I get up at 7.00 a.m. when the alarm clock wakes me up. I get showered, I eat and then I set off for work.

Pause

I walk out of the front door of the block of flats, cross the road and walk to the bus stop on Saltshouse Road. I know at the bus stop I will see the same people that I always see. There's the guy who works at Debenhams in the men's wear section. Always nicely turned out in a suit and shirt and tie. There are the two women, possibly lesbians who work at the fashion shop on the corner of Argyle Street. They are always in bright coloured boots and as much tartan as they can possibly wear in one outfit and purple or bright blue hair, depending on how they have felt over the weekend. Then there's the couple of likely lads as I think of them. They work in the betting shop in town. Always dressed sharply. They look like a couple of spivs. Probably because they are. Then there is Mrs Williams who lives in one of the flats in my complex. Always goes into the city centre on the 8.15 morning bus. Where she goes I have no idea, as she retired two years ago. Maybe she can't get out of the habit of travelling into the city centre for 9.00 a.m. like she used to when she worked as a reception-ist for a department store. Old habits die hard, I suppose. Then there are the factory boys and girls. There are about ten of them. They work in the rubber factory at the back of the station. They are always dressed in denim, as you would expect.

Pause

So we all wait for the number 55 which will take us to our jobs. I look around sometimes and think that we are all like robots. We all arrive at the same time. Mrs Williams is always at the front of the queue, behind her is the guy from Debenhams, I arrive after him, then the two lesbians arrive shortly after me, the factory workers come out of the corner shop about three minutes before the bus is due and the two likely lads are always just on time. It drives me mad, it really does. It's the predictability of it all. The council have provided a shelter for us in case the weather is inclement. So obviously it's a target for the fly posters and graffiti artists. I must admit, just to break the monotony of it all I find myself reading every poster and every bit of graffiti to pass the time and relieve the boredom of it all. I've usually managed to get there in reasonably good time to read everything. Which bands are going to be playing at the local pub at the weekend and who has been in the shelter the previous night and left their graffiti tag. Then at precisely 8.15 a.m. the bus will pull up and one by one we will enter, where we will be met by the driver, a male in his late 50s who never smiles. He looks as bored as I am. It's about the only thing we have in common. He drives along the same route picking up the same people along the way. The first stop is to pick up the school kids who attend the private school in the city centre. There's four of them all neatly turned out in their school uniform. It's alright for some. I went to a comprehensive, which is probably why I work in an office shuffling bits of paper. The stop after that we pick up a chap who I've seen going into a block of offices near where I work. He always looks important. Dressed in a smart suit and always has a copy of *The Times* under his arm. We arrive at the bus station at precisely 8.45 a.m. and we all trudge off to our places of work.

Pause

I just wish something would happen that would break the routine of it all.

Fades

Scene Two

Stephanie sits in a chair in her lounge.

Lights up

If it wasn't for the man in my life, I think I would just go into a meltdown caused by extreme boredom. I can imagine being in a hospital bed in a psychiatric ward and the doctor coming round on his daily visits and stopping at my bed and saying, 'right nurse, what do we have here?' 'Well doctor,' she'd say, 'this is Miss Randall, a sad case suddenly went berserk in a bus shelter whilst waiting for the number 55 bus. Had to be restrained from wrecking the shelter.'

Pause

I think it's the boredom I feel about my work and the journey to it that attracted me to a guy who's got a bit of excitement in him. Lewis is his name. He's a real Jekyll and Hyde character. He's got a jealous streak. He doesn't like me talking to other guys basically. If we are out together and we bump into people from work, he has been known to get a bit moody. Take last Saturday for instance. We were in a pub having a drink when in came the boss, Vic, and a couple of the guys from the sales team. They were celebrating winning a big order. Anyway, they clap eyes on me and all three of them come over. I introduced everyone as you do. Lewis was polite, but when they had moved on to another pub he started being a bit moody, saying I was flirting. Which I certainly wasn't. He can be really off with me sometimes but he can also have me in stitches laughing at his antics. We were on holiday recently and he just had me in fits of laughter. He was like a big kid. We'd be walking along and he would have to walk on a wall whilst still holding my hand and pretend he was falling off. When you've had a bit to drink that can seem really funny. Then we went to the seaside and there are those photograph opportunities. Wooden characters in old costumes with a hole where the head should be; and you stick yours in and get someone to take a picture. I've got loads of pictures of him as various characters, Henry VIII, a pirate and a cowboy to name but a few.

Pause

It's just the other side of him that I don't like much. The side that wants to control. The side that doesn't want me to talk to other men or basically have attention from any other man but him. I suppose I

40

will just have to accept him as he is. I guess. I can say one thing, he certainly isn't boring, not like some of the guys that girls in the office are going out with. When we get to work on a Monday and we chat about the weekend that has just passed they all seem to have done the same things that they did the previous weekend. Whereas with Lewis I never know what he has planned for the weekend ahead when he turns up at my place. He'll generally have tickets for somewhere. He's one of those people who can get freebies and discount tickets for anywhere. Sometimes it's a football or rugby match, sometimes the theatre or expensive restaurant. He's got money as well, he comes from a rich family. A family with connections.

Pause

And let's just say our love life isn't boring. It could be in my flat, in a layby, a posh hotel. Anywhere that takes our fancy really. He's a bit of a lad. He's also taken to photographing me. I didn't feel comfortable at first. He started taking photos of me as I came out of the shower. Then it was me laid naked on the bed. Nothing smutty. But in a way I feel flattered, he always tells me that I am beautiful. We both look at them on his phone. I haven't always had a great deal of confidence and in a way it has made me feel a bit better about myself. He always swears to me that the photos are for him alone and he does not share them with anyone. I believe him, because I know that he is so jealous of me even talking to another guy, so he is not going to share them with another bloke. Is he?

Fades

Scene Three

Stephanie sits alone at the bus stop.

Lights up

I am sitting here at the bus stop not knowing what to do with myself. Today has just been horrific. I've just come out of the police station after giving a statement and I've had to come here to sit down and collect my thoughts. I'm still reeling after what has just occurred in my life, the last three days have just been horrific.

Pause

Everything started on Saturday evening. Lewis had planned the week end as he generally does. He got us tickets for the theatre. I really enjoyed it. Afterwards we hung around for drinks in the theatre bar. He was talking to a few people, he knows everybody. He started talking to some guys he knew from the golf club that he is a member of. I was getting a little bored with hearing about exploits on the golf course. Who's got the best clubs and who did the best shot, etc. I noticed out of the corner of my eye a guy I went to school with, Philip. We smiled at each other as acknowledgement and then we got talking. It was just harmless chit chat really, we talked about the play we'd just seen and life since school. He was with his brother and his wife. We were talking away and then it happened. Lewis had obviously seen us talking and didn't like what he saw. I heard him shout, 'who's that you're talking to?' Then he appeared right in front of us. I was just about to say something when he hit Philip, knocking him to the floor. Philip's brother tried to intervene and he was punched as well. It was awful. I just broke down in tears. Then he grabbed hold of my arm and dragged me out of the bar, through the exit and onto the pavement. He then started to shout at me, telling me that I was all sorts of things, that I can't even repeat.

Pause

I managed to break free and walk towards a taxi that was parked just outside the theatre. A burly taxi driver got out of his cab and walked towards the both of us. He told Lewis that he wasn't getting in his cab. He then opened the door and I climbed in. I was so upset. I gave him my address and he took me straight there and refused to take my money for the fare. He was a real gentleman. Unlike that prat. He advised me to inform the police what had occurred and gave me his details. He said he would give a statement to the police if required. He also told me not to answer the intercom if Lewis came round.

Pause

As soon as I got in, I rang the police. My arm was very badly bruised. They came round almost straight away. Lewis made the mistake of coming round and pressing the intercom whilst the officer was there. Luckily I never gave him a key fob. The female officer dealt with it. He was just pressing the buzzer constantly. The officer said she would call for back up. Next thing I could hear a commotion outside. I heard him shout, 'Bitch' and a few swear words thrown in for good measure. We looked out of the window and I could see him bundled into a police van with its blue light flashing.

Pause

After the police officer had gone I went to bed. I had switched my mobile onto silent because I had an idea that he would try and make contact. When I got up in the morning I plucked up the courage to look at my phone. I had over twenty messages from him, all unpleasant. He called me all sorts of names and made threats. I contacted the police officer who had come down initially and she came and looked at my phone. She took it away as evidence.

Pause

The officer came round again on the Sunday evening to inform me what had occurred with him. He had been arrested on Saturday evening for the assault on me, and was duly charged. They were in the process of taking statements from witnesses to the assaults at the theatre. And also taking a statement from the taxi driver who had witnessed him assaulting me. She said that he had previous convictions and that he could expect a custodial sentence. She also said that they had transferred the messages he had sent me onto a computer file and that he would be further charged with harassment. I asked the obvious question, 'where is he now?' 'He is out of custody but has been informed that he is not to approach you,' she said. I felt reasonably assured. I spent the rest of the day just relaxing as best I could but it wasn't easy. I responded to one of his texts informing him that I never wanted to see him again, then I blocked his number. My phone rang a few times from a public phone, I just didn't answer it. I knew it would be him. Even they stopped after about 6 p.m. I thought I was free of him, but how wrong I was.

Pause

I had trouble sleeping in the night and consequently struggled to get up in the morning. I pressed the snooze button on the alarm a few times before finally getting up. I managed to get showered, have breakfast, put my make up on and clothed in record time.

Pause

I set off for the bus stop slightly later than usual. Of course, everyone else was already in line. As I walked across the road, I could sense everyone looking at me. At first, I thought it was because I was late and therefore would be in a different place in the queue. Then, I saw a couple of the factory lads giggle and nudge one another. I pretended not to notice. I could see from a distance that the fly posters had been in action over the weekend as there were posters all over the shelter. I thought I'd have a look at what music gigs were on over the weekend. Maybe I could persuade some of the girls to have a night out at a music venue in the town. I walked up and the laughter got louder and then people started to look away. I looked at the posters and I let out a gasp in sheer horror. The posters were of me, nude. These were the photos Lewis had taken of me. He must have posted them last thing on the Sunday night. I was horrified. He'd also put crude messages underneath. I burst into tears and Mrs Williams came over to comfort me. She told the lads to stop giggling and to take them down. Which they duly did. They were given to me in a ball. I couldn't go to work, I just couldn't. I ran back to my flat with Mrs Williams following me.

Pause

I rang the police officer straight away and reported it. She was great. She came round within minutes and took another statement. Of course we knew who it was but how could we prove it? But of course we had his handwriting on the bottom of the posters, and they were taken away as evidence. I felt so embarrassed that pictures of me naked were posted in a place where people who saw me most days would have sight of. I didn't feel that I was going to get over it all.

Fades

Scene Four

Stephanie sits in a hotel lobby. She is smartly dressed.

Lights up

Well it's a couple of months since I spoke to you last. And a lot has happened, I can tell you.

Pause

I was at my wits' end not knowing what I was going to do. I was the victim of revenge porn. I felt so humiliated. But a lot of water has passed under the bridge, you might say. I am in a new job and have started afresh. I moved away into a far better life. I couldn't believe that the worst thing that happened to me had the best ending. Lewis got taken to court and was charged with assault, harassment etc, etc and was sent to prison for five years. He got what he deserved. Hope he rots in there. But something happened which I'm sure Lewis didn't think would. He also put the posters up near where I work, if the embarrassment of the bus stop wasn't enough. One of my colleagues, Sue, saw them as she was walking to work and thankfully took them down as soon as she could.

Pause

However, people had seen them, which turned out to be a life changer for me. A week previously a guy had set up a photography studio adjacent to our office. He started work early and had seen them, and when Sue was taking them down he approached her. He asked who I was, and when she told him that I worked in the office he left his card with her and asked that she pass it onto me.

Pause

Anyway, I made contact with him and was invited to his studio and we did some shots, all fully clothed. He sent them to his agency and they liked what they saw. Next thing I was offered a contract. I went into work and handed my notice in. There was no animosity, my work colleagues and boss were all very understanding and they wished me the best for the future. I then gave up my flat and moved to London. I have glamour work lined up months in advance. The agency takes care of all the bookings. Next week I am in Paris for a clothes launch and them I'm off to New York.

Pause

I've never been so busy, and I'm loving every minute of it.

She gets up from her seat.

Well must dash, my lift is here. I've got a photo shoot for a magazine.

Ends